Once A Ponce A Time

Written by Alison & Joseph Vokes
Illustrated by Corby Blem

Halo
Publishing International
www.halopublishing.com

Library of Congress Control Number: 2010912824
ISBN 978-1-935268-45-1

Halo
Publishing International
www.halopublishing.com

Printed in the United States of America

To Shannon for loving me unconditionally and for being the best wife and mother I dreamed existed.

To Hillery Glasby for showing me that the only walls in front of us are ones that we put there ourselves.

To my Mother who showed me that life is a game to cherish and enjoy.

To my Father who showed me that hard work will get you everywhere.

-J.V.

I would like to thank Daddy and Momma and Lucas and Corby.... There that's it!

-A.V.

"Alison tell me a story," said her father.

"I need a book," was Alison's reply.

"No, I don't want you to read me a story. I want you to tell me a story," he said.

"Hand me that magic cup. That's magic soup in there!" (He hands it to her) "I got it!" (She holds it to her ear.)

"Not like that, Alison," he laughs.

"Dad, that's how I do it. I got magic soup in my heart."

Once a ponce a time there comed a big story box. It's a box filled with stories and music.

So we got to play this game to open the box. Hold the controller......*bing, bing, bing, bing, boing, boing, boing, boing, bing, bing, bing, bing, boing, boing, boing, boing, bing, bing, bing, bing, boing, boing, boing, boing.* Here is my friend Shanny. Shanny is Jonas's friend, Jonas is Fanet's friend and Fanet is Woobeet's friend.

THE END

And the story begins!

Once a ponce a time there wiz a beautiful princess Panda Bear named Alison Panda Bear. She wanted to live with me. I said yes and nothing happened.

THE END

Once a ponce a time there wiz a very beautiful princess. She was going to her mom and dad's house. She was flying and a bee started chasing her. She flew very high to the moon. The bee couldn't fly so far, so he fell to the ground.

THE END

"ooohh Alison, that was scary. Tell me a nice story," said her father.

Once a ponce a time there wiz a nice, beautiful princess. She went for a walk and saw not mean things. She saw a nice moose. She saw a nice polar bear. She saw a nice tiger. That is where her friends were.

THE END

Once a ponce a time there wiz a BIG bear,.....actually a little sheep. What is it called daddy?...A LAME?

"A lamb," her father replied.

Yeah a lamb! She found a big, big, big, big, big, big, big, big, giant puppy and he woofed so loud like, "WOOOOOOOF." The puppy and the lamb sneaked up. That means they're friends.

THE END

Once a ponce a time there wiz a beautiful, beautiful, beautiful, beautiful, beautiful, pretty, pretty, pretty, beautiful, beautiful girl with a bird hat on. She was gonna fly with her family, with her mom, dad, and her brother. But she had bad wings. She tried to fly, but fell to the ground. She tried again and walked to the sky.

THE END

Once a ponce a time there wiz a seatbulb. "Do you know what a seatbulb is?"

A seatbulb is a little fish that bites people. It wiggles its face and rolls its eyes when it sees.....people.

THE END

Once a ponce a time there wiz a moose, no a giraffe, no a deer! The deer heard something growling. It was a puppy and it bit him. But, he didn't know it was a deer. So, he put a band aid on his friend and they went to bed.

THE END

Once a ponce a time there wiz a huge, huge, huge, huge, huge, huge, huge, huge, huge, huge, huge, huge bee that was so bad! He was doing this (karate move), he was doing this (ballerina move) and doing this (bending over) and he got stung!

THE END

I got a longer story, bigger than a circle, a big circle.

Once a ponce a time there wiz a beautiful princess named Alison. She went down the stairs. She went in circles because the stairs were twisted. She went in circles really fast. She saw a big, big, big, big, big, big, big, big green queen.

She went away from her 'cause she was scared.
Her name wiz....actually her name wiz Carlos and
there was a big rock.

It was a dancin' rock. There wiz a dancin' turkey and a dancin' big cow and here's another one, a dancin' big elephant and a dancin' bear. He was a silly bear. He was shakin' his booty. And there was dancin' feet and a dancin' house. They kept dancin' then they got tired.

Then there was a big story end, the doors closed and THE END

That was a good story dad!

That was the best story EVER…..and nothing happened.

THE END!

LaVergne, TN USA
26 September 2010
198479LV00001B